# THE ADVENTURES OF THOMAS

Eight fantastic stories about Thomas and his friends!

## THOMAS, BERTIE AND THE BUMPY LINE

Every afternoon Thomas the Tank Engine puffs along his branch line with Annie and Clarabel.

First, they pass the water mill. Next, they come to a big farm. Then, they can see a bridge with a village nestled either side of it.

This is a special place.

Whenever children hear Thomas coming along, they stand on the bridge waving until he is out of sight.

One day, Thomas was running late. He had stopped at the signal before the bridge to talk to some new children.

Percy was waiting too.

"Hurry up Thomas," called Percy when the signal dropped. "If you're late the Fat Controller may get a new engine to replace you."

"He would never do that," thought Thomas.

But he was worried.

Next day, Thomas hurried along the line. Just ahead was the goods yard. There, on the platform, was an inspector waving a red flag.

Next Thomas saw some children. They were waving too. "Something must be wrong," thought Thomas. "This station is for goods, not passengers."

"Help Thomas, help. We are glad to see you," called the children. "Please will you take us home?"

The Station Master explained to Thomas's driver that the school bus had broken down and that all the parents would be worried if the children were late.

Thomas waited as the children walked down from the bridge. Then he took them to the next station where Bertie was waiting to take them home.

When Thomas finished his journey he was very late. He was worried that the Fat Controller might be cross with him.

"I warned Thomas," puffed Percy to James. "He's been late one time too many. He'll be in trouble now."

But next morning the Fat Controller was nowhere to be seen.

"Thank goodness," sighed Thomas.

Thomas knows every part of his branch line, but just ahead was a stretch where the hot sun had bent the rails on the track.

"Careful Thomas," called his driver. But it was too late. "That's done it," said his driver. "We shan't get any further today."

"But what about my passengers?"

"Don't you worry – they'll be looked after," replied his driver.

While workmen repaired the line, Thomas had to shunt trucks in the yard.

Bertie came to see him.

"I understand you need my help again."

"Yes Bertie," replied Thomas sadly. "I can't run without my rails."

Bertie set off to collect Thomas's passengers.

"Hello Bertie," they said. "We are glad you are here."

Bertie drove along the road that runs by the railway. He stopped at each station along the line. Sometimes he stopped between stations to let people off closer to their homes.

Thomas felt miserable. "I've lost my passengers. They'll like Bertie better than me."

The Fat Controller arrived. "Your branch line is repaired. I'm going to change your timetable so that you and Bertie can work together more."

When Thomas reached the station there were all his passengers. "Bertie is a good bus, but we missed our train rides with you," they said.

Later Thomas spoke to Bertie.

"Thank you for looking after my passengers."

"That's all right Thomas, I like to make new friends but I'm glad to share them with you."

"Bertie," said Thomas. "You're a very good friend indeed."

# MAVIS AND TOBY

Mavis is a diesel engine who works for the Quarry company, shunting trucks in their sidings. She has six small wheels hidden by sideplates just like Toby's.

Mavis is young and full of her own ideas. She loves rearranging things, too, and began putting Toby's trucks in different places every day.

This made Toby cross.

"Trucks," he grumbled, "should be where you want them, when you want them."

"Fiddlesticks," said Mavis and flounced away.

At last Toby lost patience. "I can't waste time playing 'Hunt the Trucks' with you. Take them yourself."

Mavis was pleased. Taking trucks made her feel important.

At the station, Diesel oiled up to her.

"Toby's an old fusspot," she complained.

Diesel sensed trouble and was delighted.

"Toby says only steam engines can manage trucks," continued Mavis.

"How absurd. Depend upon it, Mavis. Anything steam engines can do, we diesels can do better."

Diesel knew nothing about trucks but Mavis didn't realise this.

Toby's line crosses with the main road behind the station and, for a short way, follows a farm lane. Frosty weather makes the muddy lane rock-hard and very slippery.

Toby stops before reaching the lane. His fireman halts the traffic at the crossing and then he sets off again. By using the heavy trucks to push him along he has no trouble with the frosty rails in the lane. It is the only safe thing to do in this kind of weather.

Toby warned Mavis and told her just what to do.

"I can manage, thank you," she replied. "I'm not an old fusspot like you."

The trucks were tired of being pushed around by Mavis.

"It's slippery," they whispered. "Let's push her around instead."

"On, on, on!" they yelled.

Mavis took no notice. Instead she brought the trucks carefully down the lane and stopped at the level crossing.

All traffic halted.

"One in the headlamp for fusspot Toby," chortled Mavis.

But Mavis had stopped in the wrong place.

Instead of taking Toby's advice, she had given the trucks the chance they wanted.

"Hold back, hold back," they cried.

"Grrr-up!" ordered Mavis.

The trucks just laughed and her wheels spun helplessly.

Workmen sanded the rails and tried to dig away the frozen mud but it was no good.

Everyone was impatient.

"Grrrr-agh!" wailed Mavis.

Toby was in the yard when he heard the news.

"I warned her," he fumed.

"She's young yet," soothed his driver, "and . . . "

"She can manage her trucks herself," interrupted Toby.

"They're your trucks really," his driver replied. "Mavis is supposed to stay at the quarry. If the Fat Controller finds out . . . "

“Hmmm-yes,” said Toby thoughtfully.

He and his driver agreed that it would be best to help Mavis after all.

An angry farmer was telling Mavis just what she could do with her train!

“Having trouble, Mavis?” chortled Toby. “I am surprised.”

“Grrr-osh!” said Mavis.

With much puffing and wheel-slip, Toby pushed Mavis and the trucks back.

The hard work made his fire burn fiercely and his fireman spread hot cinders to melt the frozen mud.

At last they had finished. "Goodbye," called Toby. "You'll manage now, I expect."

Mavis didn't answer.

She took the trucks to the sheds and scuttled home to the quarry as quickly as she could.

# TRUST THOMAS

Thomas the Tank Engine was feeling bright and cheerful. It was a splendid day.

"Good morning," he whistled to some cows, but the cows didn't reply.

"Never mind," said Thomas. "They're busy with their breakfast."

Next he saw Bertie. "Hello Bertie – care for a race today?" But all Bertie could say was . . . "Ouch! That's another hole in the road."

"I'm sorry Bertie," smiled Thomas.

Thomas was still in good spirits when Bertie arrived at the next station.

"Bad luck, Bertie," said Thomas. "Now if you were a steam engine, you would run on a pair of reliable rails."

"Huh," replied Bertie. "The railway was supposed to deliver tar to mend the road two weeks ago. You can't trust a thing that runs on rails."

"I run on rails . . . you can trust me,Bertie. I'll see if I can find out what's happened."

Thomas left Bertie and made his way along the branch line towards the big station by the sea. James was snorting about in the yard.

"It's too bad. Percy goes to work at the harbour and I do his job – here, there and everywhere – take that!"

"Ooh," groaned the trucks. "Just you wait – we'll show you."

Gordon laughed. "I'll tell you what James – if you pretended to be ill *everywhere*, you couldn't shunt trucks *here* or go to the quarry *there*, could you?"

"What a good idea," agreed James. "Look! Here comes Thomas. I'll start pretending now."

Thomas was sorry to see the engines looking miserable.

"Cheer up. It's a beautiful day."

"Yes," grumbled Gordon. "But not for James."

"What's the matter?"

"He's sick," replied Gordon.

"Yes, he is – I mean, I am," stuttered James. "I don't feel well at all."

"Don't worry," said Thomas kindly. "I'll help out if you're ill."

Gordon and James sniggered quietly to each other.

Some of James's trucks were coupled behind Thomas and he steamed away to the quarry. The trucks were still cross.

"We couldn't pay James back for bumping us, so we'll play tricks on Thomas instead. One engine is as good as another."

But Thomas didn't hear them. He collected all the stone from the quarry and then set off back to the junction.

Danger lay ahead.

"Now for our plan," giggled the trucks. "Go faster, go faster."

"Slow down!" called Thomas's driver and applied the brakes.

Poor Thomas stood dazed and surprised in a muddy pond as a toad eyed him suspiciously.

"Bust my buffers," muttered Thomas. "The day started so well too."

Duck pulled away the trucks, and Edward helped Thomas back to the junction. Suddenly Thomas remembered the missing tar. He told Edward all about it.

"That's strange," said Edward. "A truck full of tar has been left at my station. That must be it. Driver will make sure it gets to Bertie now."

Later James spoke to Thomas.

"I'm sorry about your accident," he muttered, "and so is Gordon. We didn't mean to get you into trouble."

"No indeed," spluttered Gordon. "A mere misunderstanding, Thomas – all's well that ends well."

Just then Bertie arrived. He looked much more cheerful.

"My road's being mended now."

"Oh – I am glad," replied Thomas.

" Thanks for all you did, now I know I can trust an engine ... especially if his name is Thomas."

Gordon and James puffed silently away to the shed! But Thomas still had company.

"Well, well," he sighed. "What a day for surprises."

The toad, who was looking forward to a ride home, noisily agreed.

## GORDON AND THE FAMOUS VISITOR

It was an important day in the yard. Everyone was busy and excited – making notes and taking photographs. A special visitor had arrived and was now the centre of attention.

"Who's that?" whispered Thomas to Duck.

"That," said Duck proudly, "is a Celebrity."

"A what?" asked Percy.

"A celebrity is a very famous engine," replied Duck. "Driver says we can talk to him soon."

"Oh," said Thomas. "He's probably too famous to even notice us."

Just then Gordon arrived.

"Pah," said Gordon. "Who cares. A lot of fuss about nothing if you ask me," and he steamed away.

Later that night the engines found that the visitor wasn't conceited at all. He enjoyed talking to the other engines till long after the stars came out. He left early next morning.

"Good riddance," Gordon grumbled. "Chattering all night. Who is he anyway?"

"Duck told you," said Thomas. "He's famous."

"As famous as me?" huffed Gordon. "Nonsense!"

"He's famouser than you," replied Thomas. "He went a hundred miles an hour before you were thought of."

"So he says," snorted Gordon. "But I didn't like his looks. He's got no dome. Never trust domeless engines – they're not respectable. I never boast, but I'd say that a hundred miles an hour would be easy for me."

Duck took some trucks to Edward's station.

"Hello," called Edward. "That Famous Engine came through this morning. He whistled to me. Wasn't he kind?"

"He's the finest engine in the world," replied Duck. Then he told Edward what Gordon had said.

"Take no notice," soothed Edward. "He's just jealous. Look! He's coming now."

Gordon's wheels pounded the rails.

"He did it! I'll do it. He did it, I'll do it." Gordon's train rocketed past and was gone.

"He'll knock himself to bits," chuckled Duck.

"Steady Gordon," called his driver. "We aren't running a race!"

"We are then," said Gordon, but he said it to himself.

Suddenly Gordon began to feel a little strange.

"The top of my boiler seems funny," he thought. "It feels as if something is loose. I'd better go slower."

But it was too late. On the viaduct, they met the wind. It was a teasing wind which blew suddenly in hard puffs. Gordon thought it wanted to push him off the bridge.

"No you don't," he said firmly.

But the wind had other ideas. It curled around his boiler, crept under his loose dome and lifted it off and away into the valley below. Gordon was most uncomfortable.

The cold wind was whistling through the hole where his dome should be and he felt silly without it.

At the Big Station, the trucks laughed at him. Gordon tried to "wheesh" them away but they crowded round no matter what he did.

On the way back to the shed Gordon wanted his driver to stop and fetch his dome.

"We'll never find it now," said the driver. "You'll have to go to the works for a new one."

Gordon was very cross.

"I hope the shed is empty tonight," he huffed to himself.

But all the engines were there waiting.

"Never trust Domeless engines," said a voice from somewhere behind him. "They aren't respectable."

# NO JOKE FOR JAMES

James is a mixed traffic engine. He can pull both trucks and coaches. He is proud of his smart red paint and so is his driver.

"Everyone says you brighten up their day, James."

One morning, James whistled loudly at the other engines. "Look at me. I am the smartest most useful engine on the line."

"Rubbish," replied Thomas. "We're all useful. The Fat Controller says so and he's Sir Topham Hatt, head of the whole railway."

"You know what James?" added Percy.

"What?" replied James.

"You're getting all puffed up!"

James huffed away.

Later he was still boasting. "I'm the pride of the line."

"I saw you pulling trucks today. You're only a goods engine!" snorted Gordon.

James was furious. "I pull coaches too!"

"Not as much as I do," grunted Gordon.

"But the Fat Controller has plans for me."

James was making this up but Gordon believed him.

"What plans?"

"Er—wait and see."

"Oh dear," thought James. "Now what'll I do?"

Thomas was shunting shining new coaches.

"Good morning, James."

"Are those coaches for me?" asked James hopefully.

"No. These are for Gordon's express. I'll fetch your trucks next."

But James was going to play a trick on the other engines.

"Actually Thomas, I'm taking the coaches. The Fat Controller asked me to tell you."

"What about the trucks?"

"Er—give them to Gordon."

"Come on, Thomas," said his driver, "orders are orders."

So when James's driver returned, James was coupled to the coaches and he puffed away.

Thomas returned with the trucks. A few minutes later Gordon arrived.

"Where's the express?"

Thomas told him about James. "And so here are your trucks."

Gordon was very cross and so was his driver.

"Wait till the Fat Controller hears about this!"

Meanwhile, James was enjoying himself enormously.

"What a clever plan, what a clever plan," he chuffed. Then he saw the Fat Controller.

"Some jokes are funny, but not this one James. You have caused confusion."

"Yes, Sir," said James.

"You will stay in your shed until you are wanted."

The other engines teased James.

"I wonder who'll be pulling the express today?" said Gordon.

"I expect it'll be you," replied Henry. "James is stuck in the shed for being silly!"

James felt sad.

Next morning, he went back to work.

"Hello," whistled Thomas. "Good to see you out and about again."

"I'm sorry I tricked you," said James. "Are these my trucks?"

"Yes," replied Thomas kindly. "They are pleased to have you back."

James puffed into the harbour with his goods train of trucks. He bustled about all day, pushing and pulling them into place.

"Time to go home now, James," said his driver at last. "No trucks or passengers, just we two."

But his driver was wrong.

"Excuse me," called a man. "I have a meeting with Sir Topham Hatt and I mustn't be late. May I ride back with you?"

"Of course," replied James's driver. Then he whispered to James, "This gentleman is a railway inspector."

James was most impressed. He steamed along the line as smoothly and quickly as he could.

The Fat Controller was waiting and the railway inspector greeted him warmly.

"This clever engine gave me a splendid ride. You must be proud of him."

"Yes indeed. James, once again you are a Really Useful Engine."

# DIESEL DOES IT AGAIN

Duck and Percy enjoy their work at the harbour, pulling and pushing trucks full of cargo to and from the quay.

But one morning, the engines were exhausted. The harbour was busier than ever. The Fat Controller promised that another engine would be found to help them.

"It's about time," said Percy.

"I ache so much I can hardly get my wheels to move," agreed Duck.

They waited for the engine to arrive.

It came as a shock when he did.

"Good morning," squirmed Diesel in his oily voice.

The two engines had not worked with Diesel for a long time.

"What are you doing here?" gasped Duck.

"Your worthy Fat . . . Sir Topham Hatt sent me. I hope you are pleased to see me. I am to shunt some dreadfully tiresome trucks."

"Shunt where?" said Percy suspiciously.

"Where? Why from here to there . . . " purred Diesel, " . . . and then again from there to here. Easy, isn't it?"

With that, Diesel, as if to make himself quite clear, bumped some trucks hard.

"Ooooooh!" screamed the trucks.

"Grrrrh," growled Diesel.

Percy and Duck were horrified. They did not trust Diesel at all. They refused to work and would not leave their shed.

The Fat Controller was enjoying his tea and iced bun when the telephone rang.

"So, there's trouble in the harbour yard? I'll be there right away!"

Diesel was working loudly and alone.

Cargo lay on the quay. Ships and passengers were delayed. Everyone was complaining about the Fat Controller's railway.

Percy and Duck were sulking in their shed.

"What's all this?" demanded the Fat Controller.

"Er, we're on strike, Sir," said Percy.

"Yes," added Duck. "Beg pardon, Sir, but we won't work with Diesel, Sir."

Then, in a quiet hurt voice, he added, "You said you sent him packing, Sir."

"I have to give Diesel a second chance. I am trying to help you by bringing Diesel here. Now you must help me. He was the only engine available."

Percy and Duck went sadly back to work.

Next morning, things were no better. Diesel's driver had not put his brakes on properly and Diesel started to move.

He went bump, straight into Percy!

Percy had an awful fright.

"Wake up there, Percy," scowled Diesel. "You have work to do."

He didn't even say he was sorry to Percy.

Later, Diesel bumped the trucks so hard that the loads went everywhere.

"What will the Fat Controller say?" gasped Percy.

"He won't like it," said Duck.

"So who's going to tell him, I wonder?" said Diesel. "Two little goody-goody tell-tales like you, I suppose."

Percy and Duck did not want to be tell-tales, so they said nothing. Diesel, thinking he could get away with his bad behaviour, was ruder than ever.

Next day he was shunting trucks full of china clay. He banged the trucks hard into the buffers, but the buffers weren't secure.

The silly trucks were sunk.

Soon the Fat Controller heard the news. The trucks were hoisted safely from the sea, but the clay was lost.

The Fat Controller spoke severely to Diesel.

"Things worked much better here before you arrived. I shall not be inviting you back."

"Now Duck and Percy, I hope you won't mind having to handle the work by yourselves again."

"Oh no, Sir. Yes please, Sir," replied the engines.

Whistling cheerfully, they puffed back to work while Diesel sulked slowly away.

## DONALD'S DUCK

Duck the Great Western Engine worked hard in the yard at the big station. Sometimes he pulled coaches, sometimes he pushed trucks, but whatever the work, Duck got the job done without fuss.

One day Duck was resting in the shed when the Fat Controller arrived.

"Your work in the yard has been good. Would you like to have a branch line for your own?"

"Yes please, Sir," replied Duck. So Duck took charge of his new branch line. The responsibility delighted him.

The line runs along the coast by sandy beaches till it meets a port where big ships come in. Duck enjoyed exploring every curve and corner of the line. Sea breezes swirled his smoke high into the air and his green paint glistened in the sunlight.

"This is just like being on holiday," he puffed.

"Well, you know what they say," laughed his driver. "A change is as good as a rest."

Soon Duck was busier than ever. The Fat Controller was building a new station at the port and Duck pushed the trucks wherever they were needed.

Bertie looked after Duck's passengers and the other engines helped too, but the work took a long time.

Noise and dust filled the air.

"Don't worry," whistled Toby. "The station's nearly finished."

"And on time too," said Duck thankfully.

Duck felt his responsibility deeply and talked endlessly about it.

"You don't understand, Donald, how much the Fat Controller relies on me."

"Och aye," muttered Donald sleepily.

"I'm Great Western and I . . ."

"Quack, quack, quack."

"What?"

"Ye heard – quack, quack ye go – sounds like ye'd an egg laid. Now weeesht and let an engine sleep."

"Quack yourself," said Duck indignantly.

Later he spoke to his driver.

“Donald says I quack as if I’d laid an egg.”

“Quack do you?” pondered his fireman.

He whispered something to Duck and his driver. They were going to play a joke on Donald and pay him back for teasing Duck.

The engines were busy for the rest of the day and nothing more was said. Not even a quack.

But, when at last Donald was asleep, Duck’s driver and fireman popped something into his water tank.

Next morning, when Donald stopped for water, he found that he had an unexpected passenger aboard. A small white duckling popped out of his water tank.

"Na doot who's behind this," laughed Donald.

The Duckling was tame. She shared the fireman's sandwiches and rode in the tender.

The other engines enjoyed teasing Donald about her.

Presently she grew tired of travelling and hopped off at a station — and there she stayed.

That night, Donald's driver and fireman got busy and in the morning when Duck's crew arrived they laughed and laughed.

"Look Duck – look what's under your bunker – it's a nest box with an egg in it."

Donald opened a sleepy eye.

"Well, well, well, ye must have laid it in the night Duck – all unbeknownst."

Then Duck laughed too.

"You win Donald – it'd take a clever engine to get the better of you!"

There's a pond near the duckling's station. Here she swims and welcomes the trains as they pass by. The stationmaster calls her Dilly. To everyone else she is always Donald's Duck.

TIDMOUTH HAULT

## THOMAS, PERCY AND THE POST TRAIN

At night, when the other engines are tucked away in their sheds you can still hear the faraway call of an engine's whistle and the clickety-clack of train wheels turning. This is the sound of the Post Train.

One train is pulled by Thomas and the other by Percy as the loads are too heavy for one engine to do the work alone. The post is loaded into trucks at both the harbours and the engines pull their trains through the silent stations delivering their precious loads.

On a clear night, a big shiny moon brightens their journey, but often Thomas and Percy can't even see the stars! But whatever the weather, lamps along the track always light their way.

One night Percy was waiting at the junction. The main line train was late. At last Henry arrived.

"Sorry," he puffed. "The mail boat from the mainland was delayed."

"Come on Percy," said his driver. "Let's make up for lost time."

Percy puffed along as quickly as he could, but the sun was already rising as he finished his work.

"Never mind," thought Percy. "It's nice to be up and about when it's the start of a new day and there's no-one else around."

Percy was not alone for long.

"Bother," said Percy. "It's that dizzy thing Harold."

“Good morning,” whirred Harold. “I always said railways were out of date, but you’re so slow with the post you should give everyone their stamps back post haste!”

Percy was too tired to explain.

“Bird brain,” he muttered.

“Good morning Percy,” called Duck. “You’re up early.”

“No, you’re wrong,” sighed Percy. “I’m back – tired and late.”

He rolled into the shed and fell asleep almost before his buffers touched the bar.

His driver decided to set off early that evening. Thomas was waiting at the station.

"Thank goodness I've a chance to speak to you. Driver says that the person in charge of the post has complained to the Fat Controller about the delay last night."

"But that wasn't my fault," replied Percy.

"I know," said Thomas, "and so does the Fat Controller, but this post person wouldn't listen. Tonight we'll just have to be quicker than ever before."

The engines were just leaving the station when they heard a familiar buzzing.

"I say you two, there's news flying about."

"Where?" puffed Percy.

"All over the place. They're going to scrap the Post Train and use me instead – wings work wonders y'know – always."

"Rubbish," huffed Thomas.

That night, everything ran like clockwork. Thomas and Percy steamed through the stations making good time everywhere they went.

At a station, Thomas noticed a man looking cold and worried, he had missed his train home.

"We can give you a ride," said Thomas's driver. "But it will be rather uncomfortable."

"Thank you," said the man. "Anything's better than sitting here."

The next afternoon Percy passed the airfield and saw Harold.

"Hello Lazywings – are you too tired to fly today?"

"The wind's too strong, I've been grounded," grumbled Harold.

"You need rails," laughed Percy. "They work wonders y'know! Always!"

That night the Fat Controller showed the two engines a letter. It was from the man who had missed his train.

"He thinks you are both splendid," said the Fat Controller, "and everyone says that the Post Train is the pride of the line!"

This edition published 2003 for Index Books Ltd by arrangement
with Dean, an imprint of Egmont Books Limited,
239 Kensington High Street, London W8 6SA.
*Donald's Duck* and *Thomas, Percy and the Post Train* first published in 1994.
*Trust Thomas* and *Gordon and the Famous Visitor* first published in 1994.
*Thomas, Bertie and the Bumpy Line* and *Mavis and Toby* first published in 1995.
*No Joke for James* and *Diesel Does It Again* first published in 1995.

Thomas the Tank Engine & Friends

A BRITT ALLCROFT COMPANY PRODUCTION

Based on The Railway Series by The Rev W Awdry



ISBN 0 603 56095 4
Printed and bound in the U.A.E.
1 3 5 7 9 10 8 6 4 2